MIDLOTHIAN PUBLIC LIBRARY

W9-BHY-723

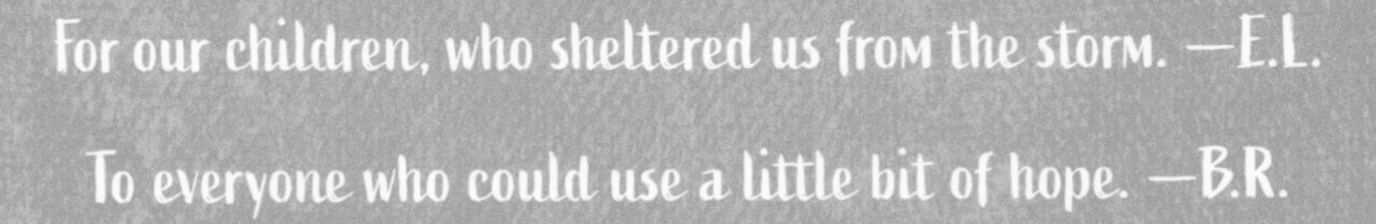

ISBN: 978-1-5460-3458-2

WorthyKids
Hachette Book Group
1290 Avenue of the Americas
New York, NY 10104

Library of Congress Cataloging-in-Publication Data

Names: Leventhal, Ellen, author. | Russo, Blythe, illustrator.
Title: A flood of kindness / written by Ellen Leventhal ; illustrated by Blythe Russo.
Description: New York, NY : WorthyKids, [2021] | Audience: Ages 4–8. |
Summary: As Charlotte watches her home and town being destroyed in a flood she sadly laments her loss, but in the midst of her anguish she soon discovers the power of healing through kindness.
Identifiers: LCCN 2020037064 | ISBN 9781546034582 (hardcover)
Subjects: CYAC: Floods—Fiction. | Grief—Fiction. | Kindness—Fiction.
Classification: LCC PZ7.L5735 Fl 2021 | DDC [E]—dc23
LC record available at https://lccn.loc.gov/2020037064

Designed by Eve DeGrie

Printed and bound in China
APS
2 4 6 8 10 9 7 5 3 1

A FLOOD of Kindness

WRITTEN BY Ellen Leventhal

ILLUSTRATED BY
Blythe Russo

WORTHY® kids

The night the river jumped its banks,
everything changed.

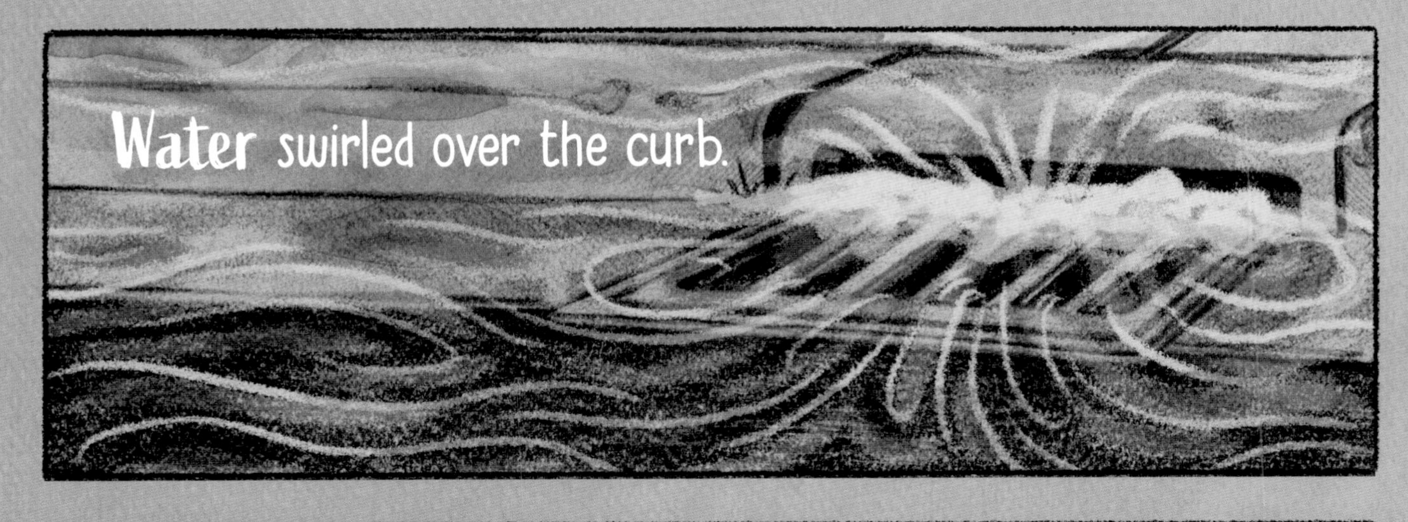
Water swirled over the curb.

Rain pounded the pavement.

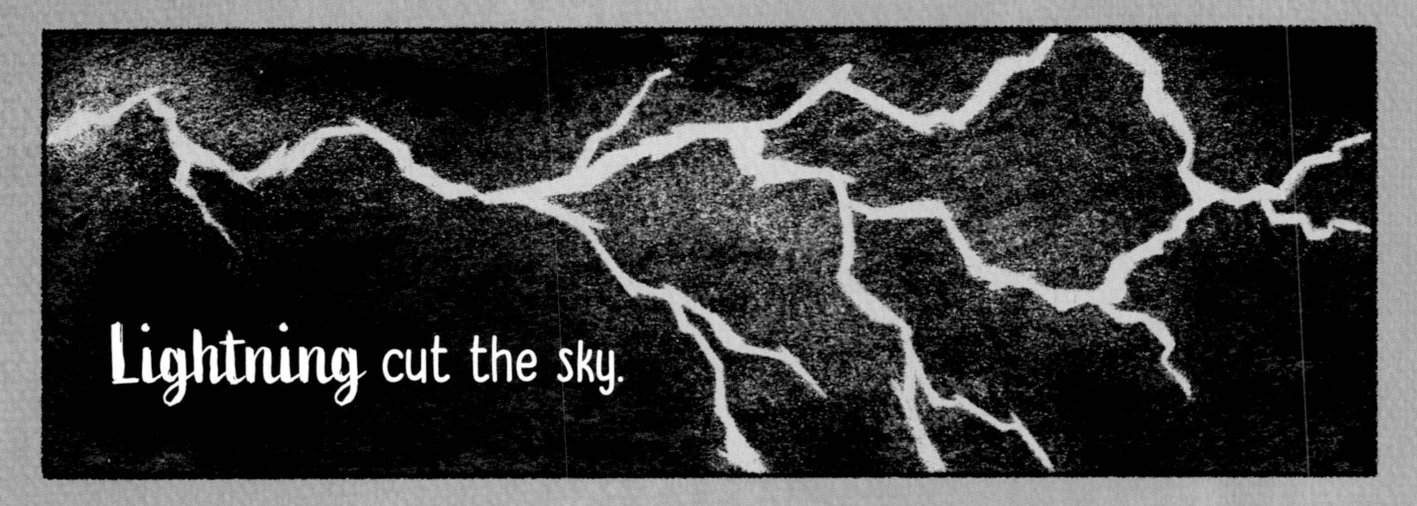
Lightning cut the sky.

Even though I was too old for him,
I grabbed my teddy bear and dove under the covers.

Still, it rained.

CRASH! Thunder rattled the roof.

"MOM!" Scrambling off the bed,
my feet squished deep into wet carpet.

We piled towels upon
towels next to doors.
But still, water seeped in.

"Let's go,
Charlotte!"
called Mom.
"They're here."

Dad lifted me into a boat.
My street had become
part of the river.

Still, it rained.

Raindrops stung my eyes.
I pulled my coat over my head.

The boat bumped and bounced until . . .

safety.

I climbed out and wriggled
my toes in my soaked shoes.

We shuffled into a building where a boy gave me dry socks and sneakers. Someone wrapped me in a blanket.

But still, I shivered.

Small cots crushed up against each other.
Mamas rocked crying babies.
I squeezed Dad's hand.
A girl looked up from a book and waved.
I didn't wave back.

"When can we go home?" I asked.

Dad folded me in his arms.
"I'm not sure."

The long night ended, but the rain didn't. More and more families poured into the building for shelter from the storm.

I squeezed between my parents.

There's no more room!

Soon, my stomach grumbled. I stood in a zig-zaggy line, and someone handed me a peanut-butter sandwich. I missed Dad's chocolate-chip pancakes.

And still, it rained.
Sounds echoed everywhere.

Sometimes a **rumble**. Sometimes a **roar**.

I buried my head in Teddy.

Until finally, . . .

silence.

"Mom, can we go home now?" I asked.

"Not yet, Charlotte."

My lip trembled.

“When?”

“When the water goes down.”

A few days later, I heard people calling to each other.

“The buses are here!”

On the way home, we passed piles of broken toys, moldy mattresses, and sopping clothes.

Someone else's teddy bear was
face-down in the mud, wet and alone.

I choked back a cry.
Whose best friend was he?
I held Teddy close to me.

Back at home, family treasures littered the floor.
Toys floated in puddles of water.
Books fell apart in my hand.

Even the walls felt soggy.
Everything was ruined.

I stamped my foot.

"It's not fair!

I want MY things!"

Mom whispered,

"We can't stay here."

Tears sprang to my eyes.

As we bumped along the road back to the shelter,
I saw people working together—
carrying mounds of wet laundry to their cars,
throwing ruined mattresses to the curb,
and clearing fallen branches.
Children my age handed out food and water.

I wiped my tears and wondered,

Could I ever do that?

When we returned, the shelter was buzzing with activity.

But I felt helpless.

Teddy and I flopped down
on a cot that wasn't my bed
in a building that wasn't my home.

The girl with the book walked toward me.

I looked down.

She tapped me on the shoulder.

"It's yours," she said.

"It's time to pass it on."

I reached out my hand.

"Thank you."

Glancing out the window,
I spied a little boy huddled under a tree.

I sat down next to him.

"My toys drowned," he said.

"Mine too."

"I used to have a Teddy like that," he said.

My stomach flip-flopped.

I glanced at my feet. Borrowed socks kept them warm.
I didn't have a book, but a kind girl gave me hers.
We weren't home, but Mom and Dad still kissed me before bed.
I bit my lip, gave Teddy one last squeeze, . . .

and placed him in the boy's arms.

"He's yours.
It's time to
pass him on."

The boy snuggled with Teddy and smiled up at me.
And for the first time since the river jumped its banks,

I smiled too.